REPAIRING THE BROKEN
BRIDGE

Shirley C. Kir

Gra

GW01606690

First published in Great Britain in 2021

by Kirwan Inspirational Books

Copyright 2020 Shirley Kirwan 2021

kirwanbooks@hotmail.com

The moral rights of the authors have been asserted.

A catalogue record of this book is available from the British Library.

ISBN: 978-1-9161077-2-4

Repairing The Broken Bridge

by Shirley C. Kirwan and Grace Gill

Table of Contents

Dedication

Dedicated to her Eagles. May you continue to soar to heights unknown.

PREFACE

Very often, when we think of the hindrances to student learning, and we seek to ascertain the challenges that impede success and that impact negatively on student performance, we turn our attention to the known detractors that are always competing for their time. We therefore seek to blame the internet and the many enticements that it offers. We inculpate the societies that shape their socialization, moulding them into characters that are total misfits. We lament the modern family structure, the absence of the support of the extended family, and the horrors of the many broken homes engendered in the current era by nuclear families that have become dysfunctional. Nowadays, we even address the question of children brought up in same-sex households. We single out, additionally, the church, and lament its lack of relevance and impact on modern day society. Seldom do we even pause to think that this problem is inherent to the very system, which, supposedly, is so concerned about ensuring that all children are given adequate education. That no child is left behind. That no child is left to languish in the doldrums of despair, unprepared for a future that promises at best to be a rat race, where each one must constantly jostle with others for their very survival. But this is exactly what happens in this story to a set of seven-year-old children, who already found themselves constricted by socio-economic factors, and issues of race and ethnicity. These were the charges that Heyler Craigs found herself faced with. It was the love that she had for teaching and for children that caused her to rise above the negativity of the system and the sinister plot that was being hatched to ensure the doom of these children.

Chapter 1

PICKING UP THE PIECES

This book was birthed from the harrowing experience of Heyler Craigs in a failing primary school in the United Kingdom. In this time of great technological developments, where knowledge is at our fingertips and success is no longer in the domain of a privileged few, this primary school, and especially her group of year two students, were on a roller coaster to academic gloom and doom. In fact the school, because it was deemed to be a failing school, needed serious measures to be put in place, or many bright and able students would end up in the lowest echelons of society, oblivious of their true worth and the difference they could make to the society in which they lived. Everyone was aware of the crisis situation of the school, yet no one cared enough, or was brave enough, to do anything about it. A plan was desperately needed to rescue these children.

How was it possible that this could be happening in the twenty-first century? Knowing of the school's reputation, it was hard to attract the right kind of teacher, one who would be prepared to go the extra mile in order to reverse the declining behaviours, the low academic standards, and what was much more important, the perceived belief on the students' part that they were nothing, and were expected to produce nothing! After all, no one wants to be associated with failure!

But of course, apart from the students, there were two other significant stakeholders in the teaching and learning process – the teachers and the parents. During the course of a single term these children had succeeded in terrorizing nine teachers! They came, they saw, they left! And each one departed with the same lament: 'These children are simply unteachable!' In fact, that was the mantra that awaited Heyler. In order to get through to them she was told that she would have to shout. There was no other way. It was the only language that they understood, and the only thing they responded to. And everyone fully expected that she, too, would inevitably make her departure.

It soon became clear to her that none of the other teachers wanted to be responsible for these students. None wanted to accept the responsibility of turning them around. It was too much of a risk whether they would come out of it with their sanity intact. Moreover, these students were expected to sit the SATS examination at the end of the year! As the teachers looked at her and wondered how she would survive, she noted the whole gamut of emotions registered on their faces, from empathy, to pity, to amusement!

When it the time came to meet the parents, she really did not know what to expect. These were the parents who supposedly wanted nothing to do with the school. These were the ones who were so angry that in their frustration they were regularly engaging the staff in shouting matches. Their dissatisfaction was driven by the need to be able to understand how it could be right that their children had had no teaching for an entire term. They were so disillusioned that they were making plans to pull their children from the school, and they simply refused to participate in any way in school activities.

So, at the beginning of her first day, she made my way to the playground to meet her new charges and the parents who had brought them. The parents were particularly desirous of meeting teacher number ten, the one who supposedly would be teaching their children for the next two terms. As she approached them, she noticed how they watched her, filled with curiosity, filled with expectation, but a little uncertain still, not daring to set themselves up again for disappointment. With a smile on her face, she greeted them. Each one of the few parents who dared to ask came with the same question, 'Miss, are you an agency teacher, are you going to leave too, or will you be staying?' She noted in their questions the genuine concern of the parent who wants to know that there are no more upheavals in their children's lives, that once and for all things would settle down and their children would be able to learn! She assured them all that she was going nowhere. She was not an agency teacher. She was there to ensure that their children would be taught. And not only that they would be taught, but with time would be prepared to take their place on the world stage. With this assurance from her, they nodded in approval, and again she saw a ray of hope register on their faces. Deep in their eyes she saw the conviction that perhaps here was someone that they could trust, someone who would put their children's future first, someone who would ensure that they did not fall through the cracks of the school system.

She now turned her attention to the children, her charges for the rest of the academic year. She would never forget this first encounter. She had heard everything that was said about them, and from what had been reported to her, deep inside she sensed that their behaviour was a cry for help. Now, as she got ready to receive them and take them to their classroom, they were, true to form as loud, boisterous, and disorderly as she had been told. She said her goodbyes to the parents, and with the TA led them away. When they got to the classroom they barged into the room and she was virtually ignored. It was as if she had become invisible. Within those few seconds something seemed to have got a hold of them, and in a cacophony, they began to speak at decibels hitherto unprecedented.

She stood there bewildered, shocked, not knowing what to do! In fact, she was tempted to pick up her bag and leave immediately! This was far more than she had bargained for! No wonder not a single one of their previous teachers had had the stamina to stay and brave this storm! Never in her wildest dreams could she have imagined that children could be so unbridled, so apparently uncontrollable! But then she considered, what would the parents say? How would they feel? They had managed to elicit from her the promise that she would be there for the remainder of the school year. She had promised them that she was going nowhere, and their fears had been allayed. How then could she now pick up herself and leave? The anxiety on the faces of these parents came right back to her. How could she let them down? Were these children not worth saving? After all, they had not become like this overnight. This sort of behaviour had taken some time to become crystallized in the students. Surely what they had learnt could be unlearnt. She felt she was the one that God Almighty had chosen to make a difference in their lives, and she could not just throw in the towel without giving them a chance. She had to rise to the occasion. She had to prove to them that they had some kind of worth!

In all her thirty-five years of teaching, she had never encountered children of this type. She had taught, she believed, at all kinds of schools, both primary and secondary with some of the most trying students, but none like these. Right there and then she made herself the promise that she would have to apologise to all those children from years gone by whom she had thought were problem children. It would be an uphill battle even to bring these children to the point where they *could* be taught, where in a classroom the correct ambiance could be created for teaching and learning to take place. She knew now that she was in for a torrid time, but by the grace of God she was determined not to leave, not only because of the promise which she had made to God or to the parents, but also because the future of a generation of children was at stake. She was determined to show them what they were capable of, to instil in them the conviction that they could be whatsoever they wanted to be. The sky was the limit! If she could only make them see that they could be the craftsmen of their own fate, then they would be able to soar above the clouds of frustration and defeat.

It soon became clear to her that before any teaching could start, something had to done about this behaviour. She was adamant that contrary to what had been suggested to her, she would not make herself a candidate for shouting. Since this was the modus operandi of those who had gone before her, and the very way in which some of her colleagues interacted with their students, it became painfully obvious to her that nothing at all had been achieved by this incessant shouting. Nothing, perhaps, apart from sore and aching throats! Children were still running wild in the school. The most intractable ones were being sent to other people's classes for a time out. That was a practice that she really found hard to comprehend. Why should she have to entertain the badly behaved students from other classes when she already had her hands full? Gradually she started to understand why that school had been designated a failing school, why children were being pulled, and why it now seemed such an uphill task to pull it out of the doldrums of failure. Definitely, for her, shouting was not the pathway she wanted to tread. The Bible reminds us that it is a soft answer that turns away wrath, whereas grievous words stir up strife. She could not answer shouting with more shouting. It would simply perpetuate the state of chaos that reigned in the school!

One thing she knew for sure was that she had to establish herself in the eyes of these children. She needed to let them know that she was the authority figure in that classroom. She had to impress on them that such behaviour would meet with zero tolerance from her! Whatever had gone on before, this was a new dispensation. This was time to turn over a new leaf. And it would all happen without shouting. She had never shouted before and she had no intention of doing it now. The children were so accustomed to hearing shouting that it was as if she was talking to myself. They were incapable of hearing her speak. She would have to make them recognize that it was that very shouting which was key to their failure. In order to get their attention, she realized that she had to establish eye contact with each child. She stood erect, and without raising her voice a decibel higher than normal she asked them all to sit.

As she let her eyes roam the room, she looked from one to another, and she allowed their eyes to meet and lock. She spoke softly through her teeth so they could read her lips as she gave the instruction to sit quietly. This, evidently, took them all by surprise. They were not accustomed to this. She had just demonstrated to them that they didn't have to shout to achieve their objective. Surprisingly they each responded. Round one of the battle had been won! They watched her closely, sensing that there was something different about her, and their curiosity was piqued. *They* were accustomed to be the ones setting the pace, *they* were the ones who were in control! Everyone knew that nine teachers had passed their way before, and nine had left! One had only lasted for a single day, another for a mere three hours! Who now was this new miss? Did she not know that they ruled things around there?

Being now the centre of attention, she sought to lay down the ground rules. She firstly allowed them to know that she stood for order and there would under *noo* circumstances *whatsoeever* be any shouting in that room! They were none of them incapable of hearing; they had no reason to scream to make their voices heard. They had no desire to make anyone deaf. From that day on, in calm voices, they would make each one of their requests heard, and treat everyone with dignity. Furthermore, there were a series of measures that would be put in place until they started to understand that for their own good, they had to adhere to the accepted values.

Even as she spoke with them, she wondered how this challenging behaviour could have been allowed to be perpetuated within the school setting. Since experts tell us that one of the primary reasons for this lies in the poor self-esteem of the students, then this would mean that whatever she planned to do also had to embrace building their self-esteem and setting high expectations for them. The fact that at age seven they could have reached this stage of indifference showed their tacit acceptance of the future gloom that others had mapped out for them. She needed to reinforce to them that there were some things that were acceptable and others that were not, and until they started to understand this, they could make no meaningful progress. Because of the plan that was forming in her mind, she felt that she needed to speak to the Principal. Doubtless she would expect that in a school there would be some sort of teaching and learning, no matter how slight. But she knew that given the fact that these children first needed to be able to identify good behavioural practices and address their concerns without shouting, she would first need to invest some time in teaching them what was acceptable and unacceptable behaviour.

She made her way to the Principal's office. She simply wanted to apprise her of the fact that for the first three weeks her focus would be on teaching these children how to behave. She had chosen this period of time since experts maintain that it takes three weeks to break a habit. As she entered the room, she saw the Principal watch her curiously, and with a little bit of apprehension. It was obvious that she felt that she too was about to tell her that she could not stay, that these students were too much for her. She was faintly amused, but tried her best not to let it show. She told her that given the fact that these children seemingly had no idea what was acceptable behaviour, that she was seeking her permission for the next three weeks to focus her attention on this matter. She apprised her of the fact that since they possessed little ability to listen or follow instructions, she would be deceiving herself to think that any meaningful learning could take place. She sought to reassure her that she was not oblivious of the fact that they were year two students, and would have to sit the SATS examination in May. Nonetheless, it was madness to try to engage them in learning when they could not sit still for five minutes!

Heyler saw the sigh of relief that passed over her face. At least she had not come to bid them adieu! As the principal considered what she had said, she somehow began to understand that it made good sense. In effect, knowing that these students had been labelled 'unteachable,' she saw the wisdom in using this strategy to reach them. Moreover, she told Heyler that because of these special circumstances she should not worry herself unduly with the SATS examination. Even though she might find a few who were able to be presented for the examination, the greater part of them would simply not be able to manage. Heyler thanked her for understanding her perspective and she made her way back to her classroom.

All the while, she was asking the Lord how she should proceed. He had brought her to this institution. He saw what the future of these children was projected to be, and He wanted to rescue them. In Jeremiah 29:11 *He reminds us that He has good plans for us, plans to prosper us and not to harm us, plans to bring us a future and a hope.* This extended to these children as well. Not because people thought that they were nothing, and would amount to nothing did it have to be so. They were no less important to Him than any of us. A special destiny was divinely created for every one of us. Her duty in this situation was to help these young children see that they could do anything that they set their minds to. In terms of their occupation, they could be anything that they wanted to be. And they could be the best!

As she entered the classroom, she motioned to them to come and gather on the carpet, since she needed to have a heart to heart talk with them. They were visibly surprised about this petition, and she could tell that they really didn't trust her. No one had taken an interest in them before. The fact was that no one really seemed to care about them. They had told them as much. She told them how much she loved children, and that she was prepared to do whatever she had to, to ensure that they would learn, and make something of their lives. At first it was clear that they didn't really believe her. Nonetheless, she continued. She apologised for the difficult experience they had had the previous term, and assured them that she could make up for it, but they needed to give her a chance to show them how much she cared. She was hoping to have their cooperation, so that they could prove to everyone that they were worth the effort, that they too could shine. They were intelligent and special. Now she saw open disbelief registered on some faces, but others started to appear slightly hopeful.

The next three weeks were gruelling. Not only did she have to prove herself to these children, but she had to erase years of mistrust that they had for adults, and she had to remove bad habits which had insidiously crept in as a result of this. Experience tells us that not only do we need to tell others that we care, but we must show them. Until this is demonstrated, they simply do not want to know what we are saying. She needed to boost their self-confidence and their self-esteem, since we are what we think in our hearts. She constantly complimented each of them, reminding them individually that she cared about them and wanted only the best for them. She didn't remember how often she planted that in their minds, but it needed constant repetition. After their confidence began to grow, she started singing to them. She recited rhymes and poems. She clapped her hands and knocked anything within reach, and realised they were copying her. She began to teach them songs, poems and rhymes, and she told them exciting stories. As the days went by their interest grew, and their eyes were fastened on her for more singing, drumming, clapping and music making. As they engaged in these activities, she was simultaneously teaching them the importance of listening, understanding and following instructions. Additionally, she capitalized on this time to teach them their tables, and drilling exercises also followed to further increase their ability to listen, to be alert, quick, and to pay close attention to what they were being taught.

They were coming close to the time that she had asked the Principal for in order to instil discipline in them. By far the greatest victory came in her declaration to them that they were a family. As they bought into this idea, she noticed how bonds of friendship started to develop. Even the two students she met who were mute by choice, their response to a school filled with shouting, eventually came out of their shell, and began to verbalize their feelings. She was immensely thrilled at what she saw happening. Now, she felt, they could start to get some official teaching and learning done!

She was not prepared for what would happen next! Call her silly, but she expected that everyone would be as happy as she was to see the change that was taking place in the lives of these students. It had indeed been no easy feat to gain their trust and to start to build their self-confidence. Everyone started to comment on their behaviour in assembly. The unteachable amazingly, miraculously, had become teachable it seemed. Imagine, going to assembly and actually sitting quietly, arms folded, and behaving themselves. And not only that, many passed her classroom daily and stopped to look in. Hearing no noise as they approached the room, they needed to actually look in to ascertain whether or not the students were there, since they maintained that they used to hear the children all the way down the corridor, from their very classrooms! Now, no longer were they hearing them. In fact, they couldn't hear the children and neither could they hear her!

She was convinced that everyone would be as happy as she was. But what reason, really, did she have for this assumption? Possibly, if the school had not been deemed to be on the failing list, she might have expected that her jubilation would be matched by other's. And when she stopped to think of it, it was impossible that in any place a single class could have constituted the failure of an entire school. The school having that unenviable distinction of failure meant that the majority, if not all the classes had produced failure! This was exactly the case, the cause for which the school now stood to be taken over by a new board of governors. In other words, the school was in transition. At the end of that academic year it would pass from one hand to another. She did not know any better than to actually give these students some hope, the belief in themselves to be able to reach the stars! She thought she was on the right route when she began presenting and encouraging the type of behaviours that were acceptable, and discouraging those that we frowned on.

That's when it all started in earnest! In earnest, she believed, since on her arrival there was one teacher who had taken it upon herself to show her the lay of the land. She was told to focus on the few who were reachable, and to ignore those who seemingly had no desire to learn. Well, *she* did it! It worked for her! It would be in her best interest to do the same! But even as she ignored her, knowing that such was wrong in the eyes of the Lord, she never had a clue what her decision would mean for her in the future. She would soon learn!

Chapter 2

POISED TO TAKE OFF

In the year in question, each teacher in the school was asked to choose a name for their class based on the theme *animals*. Many teachers there and then selected a name, but Heyler was at a loss as to what name she should choose. After all, she was operating under a Higher Authority. Her Master was the conquering Lion of the Tribe of Judah. So, as she journeyed home, she consulted the Lord as to what name He wanted this class to have. This was, after all, His assignment! He was the One who had brought her there. Immediately the verse, *'They that wait upon the Lord shall renew their strength. They shall mount up with wings as Eagles. They shall run and not be weary, they shall walk and not faint,'* resonated in her thoughts. Yes, that was it! Her class would be called the *Eagles*. On reflection, she thought how ironic that was, since these children already had so much of the eagle instinct in them. They were strong-willed, determined, witty and a force to be reckoned with. Yes! That would surely be their name! No doubt about it! That was the one that God Himself had chosen!

Now that that name had been chosen, it was only sensible to introduce to them their new name, and explain why it had been chosen. Since her aim was to practise the *politics of inclusion*, she asked each one of them to carry out research on eagles, finding out what their characteristics were. They immediately jumped at the idea! She had caught their attention. Thus, as they later shared all that they found out in their research, they began to accept that they were meant to fly high and soar like eagles! She noticed this, and she was glad, for now they were ready to be taught. They were ready to learn. Here was she now, poised to teach the unteachable!

She had often told these students that they were special. They were a smart set of students who could be anything that they wanted to be in life. And they soon started to open up to her, and to share with her their secret dreams about what they wanted to be in life. One wanted to be a footballer. He was an avid Arsenal fan. Another reported that he wanted to be a scientist, another a doctor, and another a model. And still others shared that they wanted to be business owners, pilots and the list went on. This settled it for her. They were seeing that in their own hands lay their destiny. She allowed them to know that there was One who could make this all happen. The Almighty God was on their side! So, she created little rhymes for them which would act as a constant source of encouragement, pointing them towards their destiny:

I am me.

I am who I am,

I am the best in the west!

There is no contest!

How they loved this! She had found a way to channel the immense energy that they had, for their own good. The scales were daily falling from their eyes. They did not have to be what others dictated. No longer would they buy into the negative things that had been said to them. They were not failures! They were not hopeless! The sky was the limit for them!

Moreover, she wanted to impress in their minds that they were one. They must care about each other, and build each other up. There was too much around them that was negative. They had to have each other's back as they moved forward in this fight. She taught them that they were to do to each other only what they would want to be done to them. They were to be kind to each other, tender hearted, and forgiving of one another. And in keeping with the theme for the year, this was the rhyme which copped it all:

We are the *Eagles*,
We are flying high,
Soaring through the sky!

It was quite satisfying hearing these children repeat this with such conviction in their souls! But soon the very adults, their parents, were taking up the symphony! As they saw her approach from a distance they would shout, 'Here comes the Mother Eagle!' And their faces were radiant with hope and enthusiasm. Now they too had shed the despair, and the hopelessness, that they had had. They were becoming hopeful, confident, that their children would be winners in life! And they were prepared to do whatever they could to make this a reality!

In the meantime, Heyler had set the classroom in order. Visual reinforcements of every kind plastered the walls around them, mounted in three-dimensional style. There were the phonic charts with all the sounds, and especially those that were the focus of the given week. Then there were the multiplication tables, and the literacy displays. In one corner there were the bookshelves, laden with precious books, the doorway to bringing alive their creative thinking! On the focal display there was a mighty eagle, pointing their attention to three core values of the school:

Be safe

Be respectful

Be responsible

Indeed, there were other eaglets all around the room, just so that they would always remember who they were! It was veritably a sight to behold! And it all belonged to them - her *Eagles*! The very notice board just outside the classroom had the word *welcome* emblazoned on it, and four eagles letting the whole world know that in that classroom they cared, they gave second chances, they apologised, they forgave, they belonged, they worked hard, and they always did their best!

The impact which that classroom had was phenomenal! She had wanted to lift the morale of her students, to constantly keep before them that God had special plans for them. He was ever before them, cheering them on to victory! This classroom now became the show piece of the entire school. Everyone had something to say about it. No one could believe that these children could be turned around. Visitors of all kinds came to the school and the Principal invited many of them to see the *Eagles'* classroom. They were making good progress!

Three weeks of term two had now passed, and without any shouting her students had finally understood that they too could learn. Given the way that they were on her arrival, she had been told by those on the management team that she should not worry about the SATS examination. The Principal too, as noted before, had told her not to perturb herself unduly about it since it was understood that the greater majority just would not be ready to do it justice. This was the Key Stage One examination by which children's progress was assessed. It was administered to year two students from all around the country, to ensure that all students of that age were working at their expected level. But although she had been told not to worry about it, it had become evident that there were now different dynamics at work. She knew that something had changed in the meantime. The behaviour of these children was not the same. They could no longer be deemed unteachable. This said something to her. The time of the examination was drawing near, and the external stakeholders were making their usual contacts, ensuring that everything was in place for its implementation. And then her worst fears were confirmed! Before long a date had been set. Amazingly, the very same administrators now sought to find out how things were going in her preparation of the students for the examination. They calmly informed her that all of the children had to take the examination, as provision for their exemption should have been made in October the year before. Yet in October she had not been at the school, and now it was too late to apply for any kind of exemption.

She was now faced with the dilemma as to whether or not the *Eagles* truly had enough time to be ready for the examination. This examination was indeed something big in the lives of these students, and their parents had always wanted to know how they would manage with it given the challenges that had beset them. She now promised them that their children would be ready, and moreover, that they would succeed. Now that their children had settled down, all of their attention was focused on the SATS, and all were anxious about it. All of them wanted their children to take the examination and to be successful. She now found herself sharing the anxiety of the parents, for the proof of the pudding is in the eating! There was no way that she could retract what she had told them, when she saw the pride and joy that was reflected on their faces!

Their initial work indicated to her that not much learning had taken place during term one. But then, no one had stayed long enough to build any kind of a foundation. It was now critical to stay focused on the task ahead, and to start to fill all the gaps, in order to achieve this. She realized that she needed all the assistance and support she could get. Knowing that the parents' desire for success was so great, she knew they would comply with whatever she asked. With this in mind, she wrote a letter to them, apprising them of the improved behaviour of their children and she thanked them for their help in achieving this. Furthermore, she informed them of the great volume of work the children were required to cover to fulfil the requirements for the SATS examination, and in so short a space of time. There and then she solicited their continued support to ensure that their children would be on the pathway to success.

They assured her they would do their utmost to help their children in this endeavour. She capitalised on their desire to help, and she gave the children homework twice a week. This was a bit of an anomaly in the school, for never before had this been done. Needless to say, this was welcomed by the parents as they expressed their pleasure in the fact that finally their children were getting work to take home. One parent actually came to school and thanked her for initiating the homework policy. Since this had never happened before, he needed to verify that she was actually the one who started it! Working with the parents as a team was rewarding, and a much-needed support. Every day they had questions about the homework and about the examination. Their excitement escalated to the point where some parents started to do the homework *for* their children. With a little advice, they recognised that their contribution to their children's homework should be minimal. After all, they might be enthusiastic about their success, but it was the children themselves, who would have to sit the examination!

It was at this point that she set up a table and four chairs in the corridor just outside her classroom. If for some reason a student needed a breather, she would set them to work there. At times a student's inability to concentrate and attend to the job at hand stemmed from other external factors. These were students, it must be remembered, who belonged to the minority races in the population, or came from homes which constituted part of the lower echelons of the society, and they had their own unique familial problems. She had, for instance, observed a couple of children with complaints of tummy ache in the mornings, and reasoned to herself that they must have missed breakfast for whatever reason. If she could only supply them with something to munch on! This was the perfect opportunity to ensure that they would each have their five servings of fruits and vegetables a day. She knew that she could not ask the parents, for obvious reasons. She therefore undertook this task herself. She allowed them to know that they needed to eat healthily as they prepared for the

SATS exam. She went out and bought them fruits and biscuits. From thereon, every day, they anxiously looked forward to their usual snack from the basket of goodies.

The school, as stated before, was also in transition, and this complicated matters even more. Having received the designation of being a failing institution, plans were already underway to pass it from the Council into the hands of a private body. Many teachers were therefore unsure about their future tenure there. Some feared that they were going to lose their position, and they were very worried. A dark cloud of uncertainty covered the entire institution. Little did she know that this would so seriously impact her teaching there, heightening her anxiety for the success of her students. So as she sought firstly to ground them in the basics, she was also trying, at the same time, to compile practical papers which would address the examination requirements. One thing she realized was that in the midst of all that was going on, she had to trust in her God to fight for them!

She recognized then, that overall, she needed to make learning as much fun as possible. It had to be more than just English or Mathematics or Science. In order to achieve this, she collaborated with external agencies and other people from the community. With permission from the Principal, she arranged to have someone teach the *Eagles* drumming. She had realized that as she had tried to instil discipline in them that this was something that they had especially liked. Drumming was therefore done once a week for an hour. They greatly enjoyed this and learnt to play rhymes, rhythms and chants. They sang and danced as they played. Every child had his own drum to knock. As they played and sang *It is grand to play with friends*, it was like a festival of music echoing through the halls of the school.

These periods of drumming became reinforcements for good behaviour since it gave them a natural outlet for their energies, and was a way to expel all their pent-up emotions. It also gave them a welcome break from the work. They had initiated a code of conduct to which they strictly adhered. Therefore, if any child, for whatever reason, fell back into the shouting or talking unnecessarily loudly, by putting her right thumb on her lips, and they in turn imitating her, she showed the guilty party how they were falling short. Additionally, they might hear her say, 'For everything there is a season, and a time for everything under the sun. A time to speak, and a time to be silent! Now, tell me *Eagles,* is this a time to be talking?' 'No!' they chimed in, in response.

And so, the loud speaking was quelled. Additionally, art resources were donated by a nearby charity. Together they joined one heart, one mind, and they had one goal. It was all about ensuring that the children did fly high!

Chapter 3

ATTEMPTING TO CLIP THE EAGLES' WINGS

They were all totally taken over by the examination fever. The *Eagles* were a motley group of students of varying abilities. She needed to separate them into groups, to have them work at their own level, so that she could better guide them through their paces. Her work was also made more difficult since she had no syllabus specially designed for this school from which she could work. Yes, they all did have the national curriculum on their system, but this was so wide that it needed to be tailor-made to fit the needs of each individual school. More pertinently, in relation to the *Eagles*, some were special needs students. But she could hardly say this to their parents! So wide and varied were their needs, so much more difficult the task that confronted her! Lamentably, she was informed that there once was a special needs department there, but just prior to her coming it had been dismantled. Now there were neither resource personnel, nor materials she could use.

She had reason at that time to reflect on when she first came to join the staff at the school. One teacher, she remembered, in the guise of helping her clean the classroom had dumped a large amount of the resource materials that were in the class - irrespective of whether they were good, bad or indifferent. They were all thrown out, lock, stock and barrel! This was her dilemma; these were the dynamics that were at work. But, refusing to allow herself to be deterred or distracted from the job at hand, she set about to bring the *Eagles* to the required standard for the SATS examination. She had studied copies of past papers, so she knew exactly what they were up against. She had now to find a way to condense the material into manageable portions so that the *Eagles* would not be overwhelmed. Thankfully during their times of reciting, they had perfected their times table, and their phonetics, and were becoming better and better at spelling and vocabulary. She was largely satisfied that they could build on these foundation stones.

She had thirty-five years of teaching under her belt. This might be challenging, but it certainly was not impossible! As help from her colleagues was not forthcoming, she sought help from the Lord. He was her Resource Person! He was the One who had brought her here, and He was not going to leave her in the lurch! She thought of all the promises which He had given to us in His Word. They were all ours for the asking. She reminded Him that these were His children. He had a plan and a purpose for every life! They simply could not fail! He could not allow the enemy to win this battle! These children would never be the failures that everyone expected them to be!

And so, they started to work. They were on a roll, or at least so she thought, until strange incidents began to take place. With already depleted resources, she found that things started to disappear from her classroom: teaching materials, worksheets, stationery and books. Pertinent printed information also started to make their exit. Wait! Didn't she just place a document on the table? She was tempted to doubt herself, but then it became clear to her that electronic information was also disappearing from the system. Lesson plans that she had saved were no longer visible. Resources were as scarce as gold. Almost anything that was necessary to get her job done efficiently was hijacked.

What could she make of this? She could not openly accuse anyone of deliberately trying to sabotage her, and her work with the *Eagles*. After all, she had done nothing wrong. She thought that everyone would applaud the effort that she was making with these children. She was so sure that their efforts would be commended. It was becoming too much to contend with, so she brought it to the attention of the Principal who found it equally hard to believe. As it continued to happen, she felt the need to also bring it to the attention of other members of the leadership team. Things had escalated to the level of bullying and harassment. Senior teachers would make subtle and condescending comments that irritated her to the core. At times it was not what they said as much as the subtlety that felt like a sword had been driven through her ribs. It was the deliberate, patronizing statements that drove the nail through her flesh. It was the grimace and false pretence of genuine concern about how she was managing that brought her to the point of melt down. There was nothing worse than seeing straight through someone, knowing that they are taking the mickey and refraining from letting on that you are fully aware of their feigning.

There was distrust and uneasiness, because with all this happening, and since she felt she was not being taken seriously by those in authority, who knows what could possibly happen next! Her only solace was knowing that there was a God above who saw and knew all things.

She had come to the point where she decided not to share anymore of what was happening to her with anyone. She kept everything bottled up inside, and started to wonder why was it that so many stumbling blocks were being put in her way. From reading the news in the papers she was made aware of the gradual demise of the school. On the day of her interview she had been told that the school had received a failing grade, and that it was imperative to build it up in order that this would not be repeated. The school had now changed hands. It had been taken over by an academy. This obviously meant that an outstanding grade was the desired goal. She thought that everyone understood this. She thought that everyone would understand that this had to be a concerted effort on the part of everyone. All hands on deck! She thought that it was well-known and understood that a house divided against itself could not stand!

But then she recognized that it was about much more than just thwarting her. She was not the only target now. As she had sought to bring the *Eagles* to the point of respecting the discipline of the school, she had decided that it would be good to engage them in beautifying the school; to take pride in their surroundings. She wanted them to take ownership of their school, and hence, their own learning. They had gone around the compound and areas where they could plant ornamental plants were identified. Again, not wanting to place any undue strain on the already exhausted finances, she had purchased the soil that they would need. Because she also wanted to bring alive the Science component of their course, they also planted potatoes, onions, clementines, strawberries, and lichee seeds. Her students were excited to engage in such activities. Suddenly, however, and without warning, the plants which the *Eagles* had planted as part of this project, and had taken such loving care to nurture, were uprooted, time and again! And it did not matter that some were even at the flowering and bearing stage! This really made her sit up and pay attention, for it was saying so much more when the *Eagles* too were targets of such malicious actions!

It was then she started to think, to do private inventory, so to speak. She recognized that all that was going on was not just about her. Yes, she had come to this institution, and was the first teacher that had been employed by their new employers. She was so much engaged with her students that she did not have the time to eat lunch in the staff room with the other teachers. Just maybe this supposed refusal to fraternize marked her as different. Why would she prefer to go to the playground at lunch time and engage her students in their playground activities, teaching them how to skip, throw and catch ball, teaching them how to take turns, and having a good time with them? Why did she not hang with the teachers? Did she think that she was better than everybody else? Did she not understand that these children were unteachable? Had she not been told that a total of nine teachers had come and gone to prove that their theory was correct? What was she hoping to prove? Now she understood the annoyance and the frustration that accompanied the uprooting of the plants which her students had laboured on together. These children were not supposed to shine! They were not expected to do well, far less to excel! She knew then that she had to be very careful!

The destruction of the resources she was using in preparing the *Eagles* had been an unexpected blow that the average teacher would not have recovered from. Nonetheless, there was too much at stake and she had come too far to give up. The *Eagles* would never have forgiven her if she had shown the slightest sign of defeat. Remember, she had taught them that they were fighters! They were always to be determined! They were never to give up! So, in the midst of such turbulence, she had to engage the strength of an eagle, she had to soar above the storm! Needless to say, this had slowed down her momentum and hence, the momentum of the *Eagles*. Nevertheless, they kept moving forward. As one of their mottos rightfully put it, 'Forward ever, backward never!' She had never experienced any such thing in her entire teaching career: the tension, the discomfort, not knowing whom to trust, or whether she could trust anyone. She felt like a round peg in a square hole, as if she were intruding on forbidden ground. She would ask questions and get no real answers. There was a paucity of support. She knew she was the enemy from the way others reacted towards her. She was totally isolated. Alas, this was her lot!

It soon reached a point where everything she did was questioned, and by just about everyone that should not have been so intimately concerned with what she was doing. She and her *Eagles* became the focal point of the entire school. They could do nothing without being seen or spotted. Children from other classes were spurred on to victimise them. Teachers too, were victimising them. Inevitably, they were to share the same fate as she was being subjected to. She witnessed children raise false accusations against them. They were made to take the fall for what other children had done. On many occasions her *Eagles* would cry out for being treated unfairly. How that broke her heart! But out of it came one resolve. It only intensified their determination to succeed. Her love for them grew stronger. She shared their hurt, felt their pain, and they were destined to share a bond that would never be broken!

Very often, she would go to the cafeteria to supervise her Eagles, and ensure that they had selected a varied meal, and the Teaching Assistants would try to chase her away. In the event that she stayed in the classroom to prepare work, or busied herself with photocopying material, the *Eagles* became their targets. They would incite them to misbehave. They looked for all kinds of misdemeanours to be made, and took special pride in recording them. They even went as far as to tell her that she should no longer bring snacks for them, since they should not discriminate amongst students. The aim was to give the lie to what everyone knew was the truth! These children had now become tractable! They were now the most desirable class in all that school. When recalcitrant students were sent to join another class, they would gleefully present themselves at hers!

The many pitfalls and snares that were placed in the *Eagles'* way were specifically designed to ensure her failure, and her failure obviously signalled theirs. Somehow, they needed to show that they were no better than the rest. If these could be turned around, then everyone could. The buck would now lie squarely at the teachers' door. Since she had the worst group of students, the ones that no one wanted, and they had been transformed, what was there to prevent theirs from doing the same? Obviously, they felt that it was less of an effort for everyone to let the status quo remain intact than to try to go the route of reformation. But that was their call. Her question now was how she could get her *Eagles* ready for the examination in just three months. Their success would sure highlight the overall failure of the school! These teachers just could not allow this to happen. They were adamant that this insignificant woman and her flock of birds would not make them look bad! This was all out war!

Chapter 4

THE EAGLES IN FLIGHT

The time came when there were only two weeks to go before the examination. By this time, we had reached term three. It was then that she asked the Principal whether or not she could dispense with the school's calendar for this period of time in order to concentrate on English and Mathematics. The Principal readily consented, and so she was able to practise these in earnest. Needless to say, as was perhaps to be expected, the Eagles started to get a bit nervous, and some seemed overwhelmed even, when they thought that the examination was just around the corner. She had anticipated this moment. Throughout the course of the last term she and her Eagles had rehearsed rhymes, sang songs and recited poems. She then decided that they would have a concert, where the Eagles' talents could be showcased for all to see, and especially their parents. They would finish the year on a big bang!

She considered that it would be best to leave the concert until after the examination, but she was instructed that it should take place the very week of the examination, and so it was slotted in! Moderation had already taken place and it was clearly proven that a high percentage of her Eagles were operating at the expected level. In other words, they were on stream to take the examination. The first day came. She realized that the students were a bit jittery. She had already lifted them up in prayer, so now she opened her arms and gathered them to her. She reminded them that they were ready! They had proven it a few weeks ago when they had shone during the moderation exercise. They should now set themselves to take flight and soar to success, for they were the Eagles. This calmed them and they started to relax. Nothing would now stand in their way. They wanted to do well for their parents, and they wanted to make her proud. As they got ready to go into the examination room, they did it with a sense of purpose. They were well able to do this! At the sound of the bell heralding the end of the examination they rushed out with a look of satisfaction on their faces. They were happy! They were in high spirits! One down, five more papers to go! Having completed this first day of examination, the Eagles believed that they could conquer all. That, to her, spoke volumes. They now believed in themselves! They could cast any mountain out of their way! The most important thing of all was that they had faith in themselves to be able to do well!

The second day of the examination saw the Eagles completing their Reading paper in the morning. This was relatively easy for them, because they were for the most part, good readers. They all went to have their lunch and prepare themselves, for the concert was in the afternoon. It would begin at two o'clock. By a quarter to two parents, carers and invited guests were already gathering. There was a sense of great animation in the hall! The parents were brimming with pride! These were their children! They were going to show the world what they could do! They proudly took their seats in anticipation. Out came the cell phones and the video cameras. This was a performance to be recorded for eternity! With a little booster of encouragement, the Eagles took their places on the stage. Let the show begin! Despite the brevity of the time at their disposal, the Eagles put on an outstanding performance. They sang, danced, recited poems and drummed. She would never forget the proud look on the parents' faces. Cell phones flashed; video cameras were in recording mode. Not a single moment was missed! The Eagles were truly in flight! The whole auditorium erupted in applause! When they left there that afternoon, another success under their belts, no one could tell them that they were losers!

After the concert the Eagles were returned to examination mode. Two more days of exam lay ahead of them. She gathered them on the carpet for another heart to heart talk. She wanted to reinforce to them that yet again the concert had proven that they had everything they needed to be successful. Now they only needed to relax, maintain a sweet, settled peace, and press ahead with the examinations. When the bell rang at the conclusion of the last examination, she reminded them that they had all tried their very best, and that was all that she expected of them.

The concert and examination were all finished now and so she turned her attention to consolidate all that she had taught them over the eight months and to concretize all they needed to know to be ready for year three. She wanted to make sure that they were ready for any eventuality, that they would continue to soar above the challenges of life, and conquer every mountain. When she considered that these were the students who were considered unteachable when she arrived there, students that no other teacher wanted to be associated with, far less teach, she marvelled. God alone was responsible for this. Only He could have wrought this transformation. She began to praise Him, and give Him all the glory! He had not disappointed her. These were His children, and He loved them! They would be all that He said they would be.

Even though her Eagles had come a long way, there were still ingrained habits that they were seeing all around which she did not want them ever to return to. Some were the very same habits that they had exhibited at the beginning. She recognized that they would soon be headed to year three, and she wanted nothing to stand in the way of their progress. Given their propensity for drama, this is where she decided to exploit their skills to give them some serious object lessons as to why they needed to condemn these behaviours wherever they popped up. This was executed by having the children create scenes which depicted negative behaviours such as answering back adults, bullying, lying, leaving the class without permission and running wild. This provided a great teaching opportunity as the Eagles were now able to see these behaviours that were evidenced all around as clearly undesirable, and sure conduits to academic failure. Additionally, they began to speak openly and freely about their individual roles in these activities, and noted how they were the very things which intercepted their learning, and caused them to be considered unteachable. A few of them even confessed that when she first met them, they too had had no qualms about stealing or lying. Now, however, they viewed it as being very distasteful!

It now dawned on her that this clearly provided the evidence that these habits would never ever again be portrayed by her Eagles. She considered that this kind of habit-reconditioning does not happen overnight. It involved lovingly investing much patience and demonstrating consistency of expectation. Quite often the Eagles' feelings were a little bit bruised when she had to call them out on negative behaviours. They sometimes thought that she was too hard on them and at worst, one or two candidly declared that she didn't love them. Thankfully, they now realised that discipline is born of love and that anyone who loves discipline understands love. They had finally registered the fact that demonstrating love meant that they would not be allowed to do as they liked, how they liked and when they liked. Love had nothing in common with overlooking their wrong doings. It was not centred on ensuring that they were happy at all times. She had already impressed on them that there was a time and a season for everything under the heavens. There were times that they would be happy and times they would be sad. And love was just this. It was always kind, patient, not self-seeking, not easily angered, and kept no record of wrongs. These were the points to which she would always return any Eagle who dared to say that she didn't love them, and their answers always confirmed that she did indeed love them.

Clarifying, and teaching expected behaviours, were common activities in the Eagles' class. Each Eagle was now an expert on what positive behaviours were, because expected behaviours were always encouraged while inappropriate ones were discouraged. The Eagles were now accustomed to effective classroom practices. Over her thirty-five years of teaching she had seen and tried many innovative methods but was always mindful to focus on purpose and intention. She didn't mind trying something new but to her what really mattered was the reason behind her doing what she did. So, the naysayers whose opinion was that she did her own thing, or that she was in her own little bubble, were inaccurate. She was always ready and willing to justify what she did and why she did it. It had worked for thirty-five years and again, it worked for the

Eagles. Everything was centred around the children and it was all about their success.

The Eagles, then, were at this point ready to try new things, be it new work, food or ideas. They had been taught all that they could be taught. This was the moment that she then engaged them more fully in gardening. They had already prepared the soil and planted a variety of things: carrots, onions, tomatoes, potatoes. They watered their plants during their lunch-time and it was soon time to reap what had been planted. Towards the end of June, the Eagles enthusiastically harvested onions and potatoes. It was a pity that someone had wilfully destroyed the tomato plant while it was laden with fruits!

To complete the planting project the Eagles now needed to prepare what they had harvested. The in-class learning activities were sealed by their out-door counterpart. This was indeed thrilling for the Eagles. They just had no idea how much they were learning at the same time. No one else either, had any idea how they were learning, but she did. They had become so good at listening that learning for them was now effortless. There were many who did not understand what she was doing and as a result made crazy assumptions. The outcome of her method ultimately proved them wrong when they saw the positive results both academically and behaviourally. It was a fascinating eight months of teaching and learning with the Eagles, despite the many obstacles that were set up for their failure!

Chapter 5

GIVE THE CHILDREN A CHANCE!

The question of school failure has become one of the most vexing questions with which schools are faced today, and this is not just nationally, but also internationally. As Ofsted, the Office for Standards in Education, Children's Services and Skills in the UK, the watch dog on school performance seeks to ascertain why it is that children are underperforming, and why schools generally are not meeting expected targets, it must be realized that for a school to be labelled a failure points not only to the students, but more importantly to the parents, the teachers and administrators who work at the given institution.

Whereas education prepares children to take their place on the world stage, and supplies the requisite skills they need to advance towards this goal, it is the socio-economic factors which are the first stepping-stone to ensuring that this takes place. Socio-economic factors such as their parents' educational level, the family income at their disposal, their race and their gender will generally determine their access to quality education, and will determine its ability to improve the quality of their lives. In the school in the United Kingdom which provided the framework for this book, most children were from the minority races. They did not determine the circumstances into which they were born, but yet they were judged because of this. Some parents were caught in a vicious cycle of deprivation, not having attained the level of education to help their children to overcome the odds, others faced a language barrier, and even though desperate to help their children were looked down upon. One therefore had to wonder how long this cycle was going to continue, when would it be seen that someone needed to reach out to these children, and to help them to bridge the gap and make something of their lives. All they needed was a chance. These were bright kids, but they were caught in a cycle of disadvantageous circumstances, from which they needed to break free. They needed someone on their side, who would be prepared to say that the buck stopped there, and try to reach out to them with the help they needed. Someone who would not automatically characterize them as failures, simply because they were born on the wrong side of the tracks!

On the other hand, finances, or a lack of them, is another frustrating issue which had a negative impact on student performance. It takes a teacher who is interested enough to be able to see where parents are incapable of providing the breakfast which would set their children off to a good start for the day, and with the correct heart to do something about it. The fruits, vegetables and other goodies which she took to school for the Eagles, which became a sore point for those at the school, came out of her recognition that these children needed help. Why, then, would the Teaching Assistants complain that her Eagles were getting preferential treatment and that this should not be allowed to happen? After all, she was spending her own money! But when she made arrangements to have a local charity contribute to the breakfast club, and was told by management that they wanted no charitable handouts, she knew that something was sincerely wrong! Where was the heart of love? Where was the desire to help these children to improve themselves economically, and by so doing raise the level of their family in this vicious world? These children did not bring themselves into this world. If there was no personal desire to help, then why prevent the charity from lending a hand?

It was therefore no surprise that some of those Eagles who she met in year two, who were further plagued with learning disabilities such as dyslexia, or who simply could not read, do computations or engage in analysis, would just be left to languish at the bottom of the class, never being able to raise themselves above the failure, and headed towards sure educational dereliction. Could extra tuition ever be a viable option? Obviously not! And when we think that the parents' own level of education directly impinges on the importance that they ascribe to education in their children's lives, and determines its influence on them, we have to say that this is a catch twenty-two problem! They would be incapable of setting expectations for them, expectations which are born of an assessment of their children's strengths or weaknesses, to guide them towards improvement. And so, her questions were, who then would care about these children? Who would say that this state of affairs should not, ought not continue for these children? Who would be prepared to stand up for them? Was it just a case of passing them from one hand to another until they were out of the primary system? Was it any wonder then why some students were less than compliant, rebellious even, in order to cover up their ineptitudes?

And finally, there was the question of race. Who would think that in this century, at this time, that this would be considered a factor in student learning? A child's skin tone or the colour or texture of his hair should have no impact on his ability to do well in the school system. Anyone who has passed through the educational system in United Kingdom would confess that even though it was common to say that no child should be left behind at this point in our history, it was clear that racism is seen to be exhibited in such subtle ways that this maxim was in theory only. Why, then, would she had been advised on her arrival that she could ignore the weaker students and focus on those who she believed had some kind of hope to pass the SATS examination? The fact that there is a systemic agenda to ensure failure is endemic! So, those responsible for educating, made themselves the lords of these children's lives and by so doing, set them up for failure.

Here, she must return to the role of the teacher in student learning. To her mind there is both a moral and social responsibility that teachers have in this scenario. She wants to state firstly that no one who does not love children, and desire the best for them should be a part of the teaching fraternity! Teaching is not just a profession, it is also a vocation for those who know how to love and appreciate children. None should therefore feel contented to see a child's life go down the chutes, for their failure is the teacher's failure. How then could this primary school fail so abysmally and teachers not face introspection, not examine themselves, to see how they contributed to such a ranking? Students simply do not exist independently of teachers. One must be seen as an extension of the other.

The teacher is obligated to provide a classroom environment which is welcoming, and conducive to both teaching and learning. It will be an environment where students are so well nurtured that it creates correct mindsets and positive behaviours. Needless to say, at least initially, there will be the odd student who may challenge and try to defy the standards set, but if there is positive action taken to probe behind the tough veneer, they may very well get to the root of the problem and be able to rescue such a child who is crying out for help. Teachers must see themselves as life changers. They must understand that they can influence lives for better or for worse. Before teachers can achieve anything with students, they must understand and see that they really care about them. This is a position of influence, and they cannot help but see this. Because they are largely responsible for outcomes, how their students see themselves, and more importantly what they become, they cannot take lightly this responsibility. Hers is a unique position. How many students will say that their choice of a career was based on the teacher that they had? Thus, if teachers take seriously the maxim not to leave any student behind, they will then understand what this role is all about.

When it comes to her teaching, it is certain that no teacher should be justly accused of unfair treatment being meted out to their students. Teachers qualify this since they know that there will always be difficult parents, and students too. Nonetheless, irrespective of colour, class or creed or any such variable, no child should feel left out, so vulnerable that they are always nervous, and just want to give up! Teachers know that not all students are alike, they do not learn at the same rate, and neither will they learn in the same way. They may have disabilities; some may be dyslexic. It is known that children whose socio-economic standing is low tend to develop academic skills at a slower pace than children from higher socio-economic homes. But whatever the challenge, they all need to feel that they are respected. They must feel included and have no doubt about being treated fairly. They deserve to have this chance.

It broke her heart, at this school, to hear a child apologize profusely for having made a mistake, a simple error. She couldn't quite comprehend what was going on. 'Sorry Miss, sorry Miss,' he kept saying over and over. This child could not even write a capital letter, and he felt like a complete failure. In low tones she had to assure him that it was alright. She told him she understood, he could trust her because she had his back. She was determined that she would help him. When she saw the tears that streamed down his face she thought, 'My God, give me strength to make a difference in these children's lives!' This was not a child who was recalcitrant, who was negatively affected by his peers, or whose attendance was less than desirable. This was a child who was always at school. That day it was reinforced to her how much the relationship between teacher and student was vital. The value and importance of the human connection could never be over-stressed.

In a failing school emphasis should be placed on teacher quality, as well as performance, for the simple reason that the designation of failure means that everyone has failed. Teachers should truly examine if they teach as well as they could. Do they keep up to date with the latest pedagogical trends? Have they really bought into the policy that every child really matters? Do they have favourites, and do the other students know this? What is the reason for the academic deficiency in their class? Have they sought to raise the self-esteem of their students in order to raise the academic achievement at the same time? Have they tried to make them feel valued? Have they connected with them? Have they listened to them, really listened, or was it enough that students should listen to teachers? What goals and targets have they set for them? What have teachers taught them to strive for? Teachers must never lose sight of the fact that it is all about the children!

Finally, the administrators who are at the helm of a failing school are ultimately accountable, since it is under their watch that the school received this rating. How can they defend themselves and absolve themselves of blame? To them has been given the mandate to chart the course of these children's destiny, and they have come up short. Ofsted, whose stated goal is to be 'a force for improvement through intelligent, responsible and focused inspection and regulation,' then reporting their findings to policymakers on the effectiveness of these services so that they can lead directly to improvement, did not fail them outright at the first go. Time was given for them to improve themselves, and yet they could not reach the required target. With these results being published online for all to see, and for people to make informed decisions about where to send their children, it was no surprise that there was then an almost fanatical attempt to upgrade the school. With a new Principal installed, plans were set in place to make this a reality. A Principal is a leader. She must know where she is leading her charges. She must understand the task at hand, and lead from the front. To turn around the fortunes of the failing school she must have a vision, and cause the teachers to be able to buy into this vision, and make it her very own. She cannot just align herself with the failing teachers and hope that everything will go well. She must make things happen, understanding that inability to do so will continue the cycle of failure.

But in order to chart a new course of success, teachers must be proactive. If they really care about the students in their charge, they have to do more than think that all they have to do is to create a space for them where they can feel secure, and by extension their parents will feel that sense of security. A school is about learning. Children who feel secure and happy will learn. If things at school are happening as they should then automatically everyone will be happy. Therefore, as was said before, teachers must have a functioning syllabus which is followed by all teachers at the different year group levels. They must set goals and targets which they want to reach during the course of the year. No teacher should have to fluster himself/herself to create his or her own syllabus. The importance of consistency must never be denied. Neither should the modus operandi be changed before teachers can get accustomed to it. The school leaders under whose portfolio this falls, in conjunction with the management team, should diligently work out the syllabus and make it accessible to teachers, especially new teachers to the system. Teachers must know the students that they are catering to, and tailor-make the syllabus to suit them. A school should not, for instance, get rid of a special needs department and then refuse to call students special needs students when in effect this is what they really are!

Additionally, forging a successful school requires a competent management team, a team that is capable of managing. This certainly does not mean that a position is given to the loudest mouths to keep them quiet, nor to the newest addition to the staff because they will not rock the apple cart. If teachers heard only what they wanted to hear, they would not have achieved anything. If they really want to turn around the fortunes of the school, then they have to be prepared to hear the truth, even when it goes against what they think, and be prepared, after discussion, to do what is best for all. Teachers have to be capable of entertaining constructive criticism, because it sets the groundwork for success!

When Heyler arrived at that institution, she was told that improvement was imperative. She was given a six-month probationary period with her group of *Eagles*. She thought that everyone understood where they were going, but soon it was obvious that they did not, granted the sabotage that took place when she started to prepare her *Eagles* for the examination. When she reported this to the Principal she was not taken seriously, and so she desisted from making any further formal complaints but realized that with the help of God her Eagles would do well.

Chapter 6

CHALLENGING BEHAVIOUR

It is expected that teachers will deal with challenging behaviour in every school, but this school had more than its fair share. It was always Heyler's belief that managing challenging behaviour and classroom management require the same skills. Throughout her entire teaching career, she had had the knack of reaching children at a place where most people failed. Folk often asked her how she did it, and the question always provoked deep, reflective thought. You see, for her it happened so naturally that she didn't normally give it a second thought. Before teachers can manage children or their behaviour, they first need to get to know them. Only when teachers acquaint themselves with the children they teach will they be able to understand the way those children think, familiarise themselves with their likes and dislikes, recognise what makes them smile and be able to grasp the nature of their journey. It is amazing how much children experience, and what they are subjected to, in their short lives.

Children are little people and need to be treated with the same respect and acknowledgement as adults. Yes, boundaries must be set, but always within the parameters of the stage that is set for them. Introduction is pertinent during the first five minutes with a class of new students. What is done with that time can spell disaster or delight. 'I am the new teacher sent to teach you set of gorgeous children,' she would often say, taking time to pronounce her name carefully and writing it on the board so they could see the correct spelling. The art of making children feel loved and valued is to be embraced by all teachers. She understood the value and importance of this connection and of human relationships. This was the sentiment of getting to know them and of letting them know that they were a family, the *Eagles* family, and this classroom was where they lived from nine to three-thirty. If one hurt, all hurt, and if one was happy then all were happy. She instilled in them the importance of sharing each other's joys and sorrows. She downloaded into their system that they were strong, brave and smart, and no person on earth could stop them from achieving except themselves. Whenever they displayed negative traits, she fed their minds with positivity. Statements such as, 'I am the best in the West and there is no contest; I am an eagle, I fly high soaring through the sky.' If teachers say these things often enough then it starts to become a part of them. So, every day, she had them repeating motivational statements.

Allowing children to feel that they are somebody important, even when they know in their hearts that they do not measure up, is phenomenal. A child in her class was convinced for six months that she didn't love him. In as much as she showed him love, he couldn't come to grips with her consistency in addressing his negative behaviour. No one else had ever taken the time to insist that he behaved in a positive way. 'I can't be good!' he often exclaimed. 'Yes, you can,' she would respond. She knew he loved football and that was the very incentive she chose to encourage him daily to try to bring out the best in him. Every day he did something positive he got a goal on his steps that terminated at the top of the ladder, and this signalled that he won the football that was perched on top of a cupboard. Children vied for incentives like Student of the Day, gold medals, the opportunity to feed the fish, water the plants, distribute books, clean the tables, sharpen pencils, turn off the lights, clean the white board and close the classroom door. Giving children responsibilities paved the way for positive behaviour. She solicited the support of his guardian to help convince this child that it was indeed possible for him to be good. To her amazement she received a card from him at the end of the school year that read 'To my amazing teacher, thank you for all your help. I will never forget you believed in me. Thank you for being the best teacher ever. I'm going to miss you.'

The road may not always be smooth. Sometimes she had to be quite firm with him but it was all done in the name of love. Managing challenging behaviour is synonymous with touching the lives of children forever. Teachers only have one go at touching the life of a child, and if they lose that chance they may never get another, so they must use that chance wisely. Teachers have to know when to ignore negative behaviour and when to reward the positive. Many teachers simply watch out for the slightest mistake children make to catch them in the act. This should never be the case. They have the tendency to look out for what they expect. This is the very reason they should set high expectations for the children. In so doing they would see more of the positive behaviours and less of the negative. Using their negative behaviour as a moment for education is always a better way of addressing the unseemly. On one occasion a child kicked her. This was a very difficult little girl whom no one seemed to be able to reach.

Instead, the child was written off as a troubled child and so behaved in that very same manner. Such an offence was serious, and warranted the parent being called, but when she noticed that the teacher didn't contact the parent, or mention the incident in the afternoon when her mom came to pick her up from school, she was shocked, for that action far surpassed her expectation. Her classmates, when they noticed that the teacher didn't react as they expected, took the opportunity to chastise her. This was the exact moment she used to teach her the lesson of forgiveness and the power of second chances. From that day that child was never the same again. Forgiving children, and giving them a second chance, is often seen as being weak on the part of the teacher. Yet, nothing is more powerful than that of softening the heart of a child, especially when there is an acknowledgement that he or she is in the wrong.

One can never overemphasise the importance of talking with children – just having a conversation with them. That was exactly what she did in the case of that child who kicked her. She found taking her on short walks and having a personal chat with her worked wonders. Collectively engaging children in activities of interest is a catalyst for changing negative behaviours. This itself children the opportunity to ask questions, share and take turns. For five months she had been trying to get a little boy to stop shouting whenever he was angry, but to no avail. One day, during the lunch break, a group of children came to help her water the plants. The same child came with them and asked her why she was pulling up the dry leaves from around the plants. She explained to him that if the dry leaves were not taken away, they would suffocate the green leaves and cause them to turn dry as well. With that answer, he gave her a very curious look and then gave a shocking response. 'Then teacher, it would be causing a domino effect and soon all the green leaves would turn dry!' 'Exactly!' she replied. 'That is exactly what happens in class when you shout. You create a domino effect and other children start shouting and then the entire class is shouting. That is why I call you out the very moment you start shouting.' He immediately got the *Aha!* experience. When they returned to class, she had him share with the class what he had found out. He explained it eloquently and from that day he never shouted in class again. In fact, that was the end of his shouting.

Letting children know at an early age that there are consequences for their behaviour has proven successful over the years. If they are allowed to do exactly what they please, when they please without any repercussion, then they will simply continue because they realise that they can get away with it. Once they know that there will be some sort of consequence for their action they will think more logically about their choice of action before allowing it to materialize. In her experience, many children after weighing the consequence of their action chose not to engage in negative behaviour. Modelling positive behaviour to children is the key to reaping positive behaviour from them. It is known that children do as adults do, not as they say. They are copycats, so adults need to be careful to select what they want to instil in them. A teacher must be a no-nonsense person, for once children view them as a joke or an easy walk over, that's exactly how they will treat them. This is what makes the difference between one teacher who has full control over her class and another with zero control. In the latter case, the children run wild and drive the teacher to her wits' end. This is not at all saying that the teacher should be too strict, thus subjecting the children to a feeling of boredom. On the other hand, the teacher should set the stage for children to have fun while they learn. Teachers who make their classroom attractive and interesting will find that their children will always be delighted to be in the class. It must be treated as a second home for both children and teacher. Teachers should not be afraid to involve children in decision-making concerning how the classroom can be improved. They may be surprised at what wonderful ideas children generate. If they are active participators in this conversation and decision-making, they will take ownership of the classroom, for indeed it belongs to them as much as to the teacher.

Over the years Heyler had proven that when parents are told positive things about their children their interest in their children surges; hence, the support or the encouragement those children receive at home increases. It is at this point that high, but attainable standards should be set for the children. If teachers always strive to meet children's individual needs, they will find the time to make each child feel special in his or her own way. Teachers tend to get the most out of children when they feel valued. They should never forget that if they want respect from the children, they must be fair to all, thus cultivating a spirit of trust. Honesty, they say, is the best policy. It cannot be overly emphasised how much teachers should be honest with them. To reach their hearts, teachers must be genuine. It is a fact that many teachers fail to be authentic. Teachers must be themselves if ever they want to successfully manage the challenging behaviour of children. If only they are able to say sorry to children when required and to let them know that even adults mess up at times, they will see how much easier it is to win over the children's hearts.

Many of the conflicts that occur in the classroom can be quelled easily if children are taught how to settle their differences. Teachers don't have to be involved in every situation that takes place in the class. Once the children understand how to settle their differences, teachers only need to act as facilitators of the process. Not only will this exercise build confidence in the children, but also teach them responsibility. For one thing, they must understand is that in life there will always be some time when each individual needs to be given a second chance. Heyler had proven that most of the time it is giving children that second chance that causes them to make that crucial change in their behaviour. There is no hard and fast rule concerning when to give a second chance. It is all up to the teacher using his or her initiative, as well as taking into consideration the nature of the infraction.

The home and school relationship should never be underestimated. In the hands of parents is found the magic wand that can change their children's total outlook on education. Sometimes she witnessed children soar to heights by simply getting their parents to tell them that they believed in them. There are also wonders in making the classroom attractive and interesting. That is exactly what she did with her classroom when she first got it. An unattractive classroom is a total turn off. As a teacher you have to know what makes your children sparkle. Keeping the classroom clean and tidy doesn't only give the children a good feeling but also encourages them to do the same. Once they have a clear understanding of what is expected of them and what the plan is, they are sure to cooperate, and would always want to be a part of what is happening around them. Here, giving children ownership of their classroom, and all that takes place in the classroom, is giving them the autonomy to do all they can and give all they have. Children will always be different, so it is important to strive to meet their individual needs, be they physical, emotional, academic or psychological. She always found time to make each child feel special. Indeed, at that institution, whenever a child needed that special attention it was understood that her class was the place to send him or her!

Will conflict arise in the classroom? Yes, but children are taught how to settle their differences. Some teachers believe that they are the ones to sort out every conflict, but if we always do that for the children, they will never learn how to avoid them. It is true that prevention is better than cure. So, if children are taught how to fix their differences, they will also learn naturally how to prevent conflicts. If only teachers learn to be fair to all the children, that in itself will assist in cultivating trust. Once children trust their teacher, they will be more prone to be open-minded and honest. Most teachers find it difficult to be authentic. They prefer to give a false impression of who they really are, and then expect the children they teach to be honest with them. Children can see when their teacher is genuine, and some are brave enough to verbalise it. When the classroom becomes a student-friendly environment, teachers are more at liberty to let children know that at times even adults make mistakes.

Acknowledgement of this makes it easier for teachers to say sorry to children when required, and in turn children will also find it more natural to do the same.

It is imperative to understand, as mentioned before, that managing challenging behaviour is part and parcel of classroom management, which cannot be separated from your role as a teacher. Ineffective classroom management walks hand in hand with ineffective teaching. The most successful teachers are those who are good managers of their classroom. In that particular school, it seemed to be the norm for teachers to send their children who were displaying challenging behaviour to another class. This solves the problem temporarily, but in the long run the core of the problem still exists. Until the problem is dealt with at its root it will always be present within the classroom. But she was certain that just as good practices are being implemented to raise the standard in teaching, they can also be implemented to raise the standard in classroom management. In former times, no teacher was able to gain the teacher qualification status unless they were equipped to manage their classroom, but over the years there seems to have been a lapse in this area. Heyler dared to say that classroom management was achievable, provided that the teacher loved teaching and loved children.

Chapter 7

POLITICS WITHIN THE SCHOOL SETTING

To strive to be an effective teacher, the best teacher you can be, is not a cup of tea. It can be heart-wrenching, not because the work is too difficult or the children are unmanageable, but simply because of school politics. You know your work. You know what you want to do. You know how to get it done, yet other people's desires, preferences and feelings tend to take priority, leaving you feeling handicapped. If there is not a set plan of where the school is at a given point, where management wants the school to go and how to get there, then this would set an open stage for a display of varied styles and preferences. This in itself can spell retardation of progress, confusion and stress.

Many times, Heyler wanted to throw in the towel, but when she considered that this assignment was divinely orchestrated she had no choice but to hold on. When she recognised that on her own she had no strength to stand against opposition, she resorted to what she did best - pray for strength and patience. Despite the obstacles, she continued to work diligently, achieving success as the children progressed. When it became evident that she was progressing despite the fact that she was not receiving the necessary support required, colleagues decided to cripple any further success by joining forces to weaken her effort. It was amazing how gladly they gathered together against her to frustrate her purpose from the onset of the new school year.

When she received an email informing her that all her lovely things in her classroom would be 'ripped down and destroyed and she needed to rescue them,' she thought at first it was some kind of a sick joke. The more she read the email, the more it became evident to her that this could be possible, but the irony of it all was that it was common knowledge that it was impossible for her to accede to the request at that time. It was heart-wrenching on her return to school to see the condition of the classroom she had meticulously prepared before the holidays. There was total destruction in her classroom. Displays were ripped down; teaching resources were missing and furniture was defaced. Anything that could have been damaged was dismantled, ruined, scattered and scratched. There were no words to describe her feelings. What made it worse was that everyone she saw during the first week asked the same question about the destruction of her classroom; the constantly annoying statement, 'I heard about what they did to your classroom.' Now, the question was, 'Who are *they*?' She could only equate *they* with a cross-section of colleagues from every department of the work place. *They* had plotted to dampen her spirit, to discourage her, and by so doing stop her progress. They simply did not want a repetition of the success that she had garnered the previous year. No! They would not have it.

It did not stop there. They generated accusations against her. '*She* is in her own little bubble,' they said. '*She* is not teaching the children anything.' '*She* does her own thing. No one knows what she is doing but she always get results.' They complained that she loved the children and that her classroom was attractive. To them it was inconceivable that a class of children branded as unteachable was able to blossom in such a short period of time. Again, it was inconceivable that children who created havoc for an entire year were able to behave very well in her class for a whole afternoon session. 'What was *she* doing to command these positive changes?' 'Why couldn't *they* do it themselves?' Well, guess what! She had been given a divine assignment to touch lives in positive ways, so the naysayers needed to ensure that it did not happen. What they failed to understand was the fact that her success was not generated by anything she could do by, or of herself, but only by the help of God. He is the only One who can give success. And the sooner they recognised this, was the sooner that success would come their way.

The negative attitude of some colleagues is worth mentioning, for this is one of the main reasons people leave their place of work. When there is hidden discrimination and intolerance of a person, just because they are different, this is unacceptable. In this life there will always be differences, be it in appearance, personality, race, class or creed. We have to learn to accept people for who they are, and not judge or marginalize them. If everyone were to act the same, dress alike, behave alike and think alike then it would create a boring world, for if individuals are not encouraged to be themselves, then there will be a lack of variety. That is exactly how the work place was when she started. The moment you are yourself, and do not conform to the predominant habits and customs of the so-called *crowd,* you are treated differently, isolated and bullied. It is much nicer to show a simple act of kindness to a new teacher than to walk away and judge that person. If teachers find it so difficult to accept a colleague who is deemed different, then how likely would they be to be able to reach a child who is different, and more so, encourage other children to accept that child. It is natural for children to copy the behaviour of adults. Any school where the majority of children are fighting and quarrelling is a clear indication of adults in that school doing the very same thing. If teachers are loving and kind, then children will automatically be loving and kind. How possible is it to change the behaviour of children without first changing the behaviour of the adults around them? Frankly speaking, it is quite easy to tell that politics are operating in a school setting once there is a fast turnover of workers. It is obvious that people would use just about any excuse to get away from politics and septic environments.

When there is a clear division between staff members, it can grow into a case of bullying. Many people experience bullying in their work place, but do not speak out because of fear of being victimized. Sometimes the attacks are too subtle, and seemingly petty, to warrant being mentioned. When this bullying behaviour is allowed to continue over a period of time, the victim suffers fear of being branded as a complainer if she continues to speak about it.

Sometimes it is difficult to recognise what is actually happening to you because of its subtlety. In a case like this it causes you to doubt yourself to the point that you begin to call your sanity into question. Bullying of every sort exists and unless those in authority send a clear message that it will not be tolerated, it will go unnoticed and unchecked. If management is in collusion with the wrong doing it becomes even more stressful. Hence, individuals suffer silently, enduring unnecessary stress and depression on a daily basis. This further puts victims in a negative state of mind and dampens their desire to turn up to work.

It is quite obvious that many people in work places tend to work just for the money, not caring to make any effort to carry out their duties efficiently. Plainly speaking, they lack dedication and commitment. Yet when they see someone performing their duties efficiently and successfully, they try everything within their power to undermine and halt their progress, and create confusion. The main cause of this bullying behaviour stems from jealousy, covetousness and discrimination. To a lesser degree, this behaviour at times seems to be motivated by sheer wickedness. When people are threatened by the ability of others and know their own lack of competence, discrimination and bullying reap havoc.

The most horrific part of this ordeal is when people in authority pretend to be helping the situation, when in actuality they are fuelling it. There is nothing more demeaning and demoralizing than when what is going on is so obvious to you, and people think you are so stupid to be oblivious of what they are doing. There seemed to be a spirit of evil, chaos and confusion which abounded in this specific school, and which was intent on procuring the failure of the students. When Heyler considered how she managed to overcome all these hurdles, she realised that the reason she didn't cave in was her deep desire to make a difference in the lives of the disadvantaged children.

School politics has a lot to do with the way resources are distributed. Resources were given to a class of higher ability children and were actually taken away from her class with SEN children. It is the same rule regarding the placing of teaching assistants. Heyler Craigs' class wasn't considered a priority when assigning teaching assistants. Selected teachers, particularly the most senior ones, were allowed to choose, and she was stuck with the remaining ones. When Teaching Assistants refuse to follow the directives of teachers and turn simple issues into gossip, that too, is clear evidence of school politics. When there are constant changes to the lesson planning format as well as the curriculum this also is an indicator of politics at work. When the needs of children are not a priority, this too is a sign. It is important that a school effectively caters for the needs of the children. The top-down approach relating to teaching and learning, was not as effective as it could have been using a bottom-up approach, where teachers are allowed to discuss and make decisions together as a team rather than one or two individuals at the top making final decisions as to what is taught.

More focus was placed on positions of authority and bureaucracy than on actually teaching the children. When there is a lack of proactive planning, everything will eventually be done on hindsight. When staff meetings are not deemed meaningful, and everything is being fixed or patched up as they go, this is a clear indication of school politics which leaves no room for unity, understanding and cooperation. For positive change to be effectively brought about in any school, then negative habits, customs and culture must be done away with.

Chapter 8

BRINGING IT ALL TOGETHER

The Deputy Head could hardly wait to bring her plan to fruition, so she blurted out, 'Next term the whole school will have the Heyler Craigs' fever!' This meant that all the teachers would be emulating Heyler Craigs. Heyler can still hear these words ringing in her ears. Much attention had been paid to the way in which she approached her teaching duties, and the success which had been derived from it as a consequence. It was said that the parents wanted what they had seen in her replicated in all the teachers. Now, apparently, it was deemed fitting that all should come on board, so that together the entire staff could examine their strengths and weaknesses, and see how they could work for the success of all students. At least, this was her interpretation of what had been said to her.

The staff parted company for the Summer Holidays, with the understanding that a team of four would attend a session during the last week, with the intention of discussing and fine tuning the proposal for a Positive Behaviour Support that would take a whole school approach. This was projected to be adopted in the coming academic year. Together with a visiting consultant, and selected teachers from across the six schools in the Trust who were meant to be participants, this group met on the last two days of the summer break. They tried to pool their resources for a programme which would be followed in an attempt to harness the energies of children and to channel them into the appropriate behaviours which were imperative for success. Positive behavioural support, is what this school needed!

It's a new school year and because of the intractable students whom she had inherited during the previous year, she had quickly recognized the close similarity and realized that before any academic work could be done, she would first need to address their delinquent behaviour. With the conviction that it took three weeks to make or break a habit, she had directed all of her energies into the task of setting the ambience for the right behaviour which would be the catalyst for preparing the foundation for learning. In view of the constant shouting which went on all around her, and her resolve that she would under no circumstances whatsoever be party to such, she made it her business to inform the administration of her plans, since they were not to believe that she was simply wasting time, as some teachers thought she was. So, with their approval, she started to put in place her plan to reform her new set of *Eagles*, to help them to understand that like their namesake they too could overcome any challenge, to soar high on the wings of success. And now this was what the administrators believed that teachers needed to invest their time in, as they strategized on a whole school approach to the best way to turn around unwanted behaviours, and to engender an atmosphere of calm in a place where pandemonium reigned.

As the consultant stood to share with colleagues the way forward, there was a general air of expectation on the part of those from her school. Having been new to the school and witnessed the seasoned teachers shouting at the children, and the wild and outrageous behaviour of the latter, they were genuinely interested in the secret of eradicating former behaviours and setting their charges up for success. This consultant she had met at their school previously. She had been contracted by the school the previous year, and there was great hope that with her help the school could be turned around. The consultant had previously visited her class, and had been quite approving of the techniques which she employed to bring her students from a general state of hopelessness, to the conviction that they were masters of their own fate, and that they and *they alone,* could determine its success or failure. Before she started the seminar that morning, she allowed Heyler Craigs to know that she would be drawing on the concepts and strategies that she had seen her use in her classroom. A variety of pictures and scenarios were used that were quite beneficial to their own situation, including strategies and ideas gleaned from her classroom as well as things from the consultant's homeland which were felt would be useful in this context. In fact, she made it quite clear, that she could not transpose wholesale what was done in her own country to make it fit the U.K. model. Immediately following her presentation, participants would break up into small groups for discussion, and then they would present their findings in a plenary session.

The first aspect of the presentation was the focus on how teachers should set up their classrooms to create an ambience which would ensure that students would be happy to be there. Participants needed to know that the onus was on them to be creative enough to imagine what it was that would appeal to their respective charges. Not only was the classroom supposed to be a place where teaching and learning took place, but also a place where students felt wanted, loved and appreciated. In essence, participants needed to know that students were sharp enough to perceive when these attributes were lacking, and their consequent behaviour would be the proof as to how successful they were to make this the reality of their given classrooms.

How could it therefore be that the method of choice in communicating with these students was via shouting? Was it any surprise therefore that shouting would engender shouting, and that because they felt unloved and unappreciated, they would be less than compliant to do what was asked of them? Heyler Craigs sat there and thought to herself, how many times had deviant students been sent to her classroom? This was a practice she could not understand, as to why her colleagues had developed the habit of sending students to other classes for a *time out*. Personally, she heard some of these students quarrelling with each other as to who should come to her classroom. They all wanted to be there! The general attractiveness of the classroom was therefore the fundamental concern of the consultant. It was the pillar upon which everything else would be built. And their efforts could not be hidden in the nods of approval which they would get from students who genuinely loved the space that was created for them and set up with them in mind.

The focus then shifted to relationships. How should a successful teacher relate to his or her students? How should a teacher treat the students in his or her care? After all, students too were people, *real* people. They had the same emotions as adults. They sensed acceptance or rejection. No one could deceive them, or make them open up to someone that they distrusted. Teachers had to be there for them, to let them know that whatever they were going through they mattered to them. Whatever the challenge with which they were confronted they could feel reassured that teachers were there to help them through it. Teachers therefore, had to create strategies to help children to respond positively to them, but they should be mindful that trust was imperative. Only if children trusted teachers would they be minded to let teachers know what was troubling them.

As the consultant proceeded to chart the course to transform their school, she next turned her attention to music and drama. Where do drama and music come into play in the educational development and success of children? Especially in an environment where the intention was to eclipse less than acceptable behaviour, these were very important by virtue of the fact that they were channels of stress and emotional release. As she pointed out, the way that disadvantaged children experience school is hinged on the richness of the curriculum teachers provide them. These children may never have had access to private music or drama lessons and other out of school activities that more advantaged children take for granted. In her own *Eagles'* class, as she recollected, she had already introduced them to drumming lessons, and her reason for doing this was to provide them with ample opportunities to sing and dance during her time with them as a form of enjoyment and relaxation. This had all culminated in a concert for parents and friends. Now she sat there hearing the consultant applaud the positive benefits of music to the psyche and well-being of children, she reminisced on the air of exhilaration which overtook her *Eagles* as they drummed and sang to their hearts' content.

In fact, such was the impression that this made on those teachers present at the seminar, that it was decided that there would be a whole school performance at the beginning of the new school year. If teachers wanted their children to beam with delight, then they should be given access to stress and emotion busters. For this period was a time when teachers would get to see the true character or reflection of each child. They would realise that they all have a soft and loving side to them. They would see their need and desire for affirmation, reassurance, love and acceptance. The teachers, she reiterated, should know the value of allowing the children to be responsible. Allowing them to walk up and down the stairs during break and lunch time would provide extra time to demonstrate their responsibility. But, as she pointed out, this had implications for the individuality and personality of teachers. How far was a teacher willing to go to ensure that children maintained desirable behaviours? Some teachers, she noted, did not have the patience or persistence to follow through with a particular concept or skill, and she concluded that the crux of the whole matter was that children really need teachers who were both committed and dedicated, who were prepared to make a sacrifice for the care and well-being of the children in their charge.

Another concept not overtly discussed by the consultant, but one for which she had given Heyler Craigs kudos in the past year, was engaging the students in beautifying their environment. This hands-on experience, she concurred, would provide them with the requisite life skills for positive interaction with others. Moreover, the sense of calm, tranquillity and accomplishment which enveloped them as they dug, planted, watered and took care of their environment, was second to none for its possibility of showing them that it was better to pool their resources together to effect positive change, rather than to fight and quarrel all the time, which could lead to trouble with the law in time to come.

Another technique which the consultant had applauded was setting boundaries, and together with this the importance of following through with consequences, which would ensure compliant behaviour. This, Heyler Craigs smiled about, since it was viewed by some adults as her giving threats to the students. But what they seemingly missed was that just as important as giving bundles of praise and compliments for appropriate behaviour, the same was necessary when children behaved in an unseemly fashion. This was all a part of positive communication with children. There must be a balance. Teachers had to understand that they needed to zero in on negative behaviour in an appropriate time. According to the nature of the offence some things might be dealt with right on the spot while others would have to wait for a more suitable time to be addressed. Either way, negative behaviours had to be dealt with. Teachers needed to be honest with the children, for they always got the best results when they were upfront with their charges concerning issues that would affect others or themselves. Thus, as important, was a reward system for children with challenging behaviour, one that is displayed in an attempt to help them curb unacceptable behaviour, and understand why they needed to conform to the status quo.

For Heyler Craigs personally, one thing that she welcomed most of all that was discussed, was that teachers had to practise what they preached. Was it right to expect children to be honest, fair, caring and kind when teachers themselves were not? Teachers should be able to naturally model these qualities to the children. Craigs, personally, had zero tolerance for lies and therefore, spoke the truth and set high expectations for children to be honest and trustworthy. Thus, by instilling in children the value of hard work, dedication and determination to succeed, they would see that success lay within their reach.

All they needed to do was to set goals, and strive to attain them. Through the help of God they could do all things!

The new school year started off with a blast. It was time for the new approach to be introduced to the staff who readily accepted it. They understood and agreed that for this to work there would have to be a whole school approach. Every man must put his hand and heart to the plough. What followed for the next two weeks was singing, poetry, drama and play. Children got to show what was buried deep inside. Class by class children did their performance. Their talents were phenomenal. Day by day, week by week the process was monitored closely. Data was collected on how the children's behaviour was improving and showed that it was making steady progress. The children started feeling good about themselves as they were complimented and praised for every positive deed or action. For the first time Heyler Craigs was not fearful of being knocked over at the door by galloping children. On the contrary, like her Eagles, they were holding the door for her to pass through and when it was her turn to hold the door, she would actually hear a thank you, which was like a breath of fresh air. Previously words such as please and thank you were rare as gold dust.

It was now quite a sight to behold! Teachers who afore time had not a word of commendation for students, were now engaging them in conversation, assisting them at dinner time, and were to be found on the playing field conducting meaningful activities. Children were now being recognised as individuals in their own right. What is clear is that it takes time for an entire school to turn around, since it involves a variety of individuals and personalities. And whereas old habits are hard to break, especially the ones pertaining to customs and culture, yet, with consistency of effort, there is hope.

Chapter 9

ALL IS WELL THAT ENDS WELL

Despite all of Heyler Craigs' effort, expertise, knack for delivering first-class teaching to children, and willingness to share her skills and knowledge with her colleagues, despite the fact that she was getting results and the Year Group was achieving both behavioural and academic success, things for the school as a whole were not fairing too well. Too often was she brought to the mind-rocking reality of the difficulty management was experiencing in getting all the teachers on board. It was not enough for one Year Group to be flourishing while the others struggled. It was obvious that teachers were not willing to change. Could it be that it was too much for them to go the extra mile? Yet they didn't want this to be exposed, which became a breeding ground for opposition. There was a need for alignment across the board, but the magnitude of the imbalance was too great. Teachers, as a result, were sent to other schools to garner ideas to integrate into their classrooms. Every new idea they saw was implemented on their return. All these changes became chaotic. So many different things were tried within a space of seven months but nothing seemed to be working across the board.

By this time, management probably thought that if they couldn't get the majority to start producing results, then it would be easier to get the minority to join with the majority. Obviously, there must be some kind of uniformity. Everyone should be doing the same thing. Everyone should be getting results or no one should. There was talk of a structural change and before long there was change. Teachers and Teaching Assistants became disillusioned when they learned they had to reapply for their positions. There was gossip, much gossip, among teachers, teaching assistants, principals and parents. Even children got caught up in the *I say, he say, they say*. Teachers and Teaching Assistants were leaving, new ones were coming in, parents were pulling their children. A large number of children reverted to their former ways. There was more chaos. Then there was a sudden change of direction, and, as it stands today, that once mainstream school is now a Special Education School – a school for children with trauma.

It was obvious that the plan was to get rid of all staff members who were on contract and to hire Agency teachers. In that way they would achieve their goal of saving the school money while simultaneously, satisfying their thirst for control, and their morbid desire to hammer every staff member into submission. In fact, this had become their driving force. In their view, it was easier for them to get rid of those who refused to jump at the sound of a gun without facing any legal ramification. It therefore came as no surprise that it all ended in a number of court cases initiated by the staff which they won. Additionally, other such cases were still pending. Never in her life had Heyler Craigs witnessed such blatant demoralization, such schemozzle experienced by so many teachers within such a short, two-year span. In hindsight, she has realised that the school leaders had a nefarious agenda: to destroy anyone who would dare stand in their way.

While Heyler Craigs stayed at the school just long enough to transform the lives of two groups of children, the success of a Year Group, while it can, and must be applauded, must ultimately act as a catalyst for a whole school change. Nonetheless, she found that the whole situation could be argued from a dual perspective. One was that change was not realized because the teachers refused to build a common purpose. Secondly, it was impossible to achieve change because no matter how hard the teachers strived for it, the school leaders were preventing it through their manipulative game of dividing and conquering. This pertinent fact, they were initially ignorant of. Knowing why there is a need for change, we might add, always leads to clarifying what is to be changed. This is followed by the knowledge that 'I' can change and by demonstrating the willingness to do so. On the other hand, the success of a school to a great extent, lies at the feet of the Principal. He or she must be the one who fuels this change, and channels the energies of all concerned to buy into his or her vision, and so fulfil it. Sadly, it is ironic to say that success had different meaning for the Principal and her leadership team, the teachers and Heyler Craigs. However, things didn't have to end that way, as there was every opportunity to transform that failing school into a successful one. Had it been viewed as a journey and not a destination, change would have been well on its way.

The struggles, the effort, the time, the energy, was it worth it?

'Yes, it was!' replied Heyler Craigs. 'The joy, the new learning, the smiles, the confidence, the awareness, the elation the Eagles felt when they found out that about eighty percent of them had been successful in the SATS, the growth and development they experienced were worth all the stress.'

And yet, the end could have been very different. This could have been a successful primary school in the community, lighting a fire of excellence and progress in children so they could thrive in a challenging society. But no, that was not what the powers that be wanted. Forget about what the children, parents, teachers and community wanted. *They* wanted yet another school to add to their reservoir of Special Education Schools. And sure as the sun, they got it.

Printed in Great Britain
by Amazon

75285245R00064